AuthorHouse™
1663 Liberty Drive
Bloomington, IN 47403
www.authorhouse.com
Phone: 1 (800) 839-8640

Published by AuthorHouse 02/28/2018

ISBN: 978-1-5462-2986-5 (sc)
ISBN: 978-1-5462-2985-8 (e)

Library of Congress Control Number: 2018902288

Print information available on the last page.

Any people depicted in stock imagery provided by Getty Images are models,
and such images are being used for illustrative purposes only.
Certain stock imagery © Getty Images.

This book is printed on acid-free paper.

Because of the dynamic nature of the Internet, any web addresses or links contained in
this book may have changed since publication and may no longer be valid. The views
expressed in this work are solely those of the author and do not necessarily reflect the
views of the publisher, and the publisher hereby disclaims any responsibility for them.

authorHOUSE®

This Book is Dedicated to
My Big Happy Family….
The Haq's, The Pasha's, The Wells', The Hatchett's, The Burgesses.
St. Croix's Sun, All My Beautiful friends, Seattle's Rain
And all of the
Amazingly Wonderful, Smart, Happy Children In our Family; and Everywhere! (m.a.)
I love you Mom and Dad ~ I finally did it! xoxoxo
What a Fun Journey!

Vania is a busy wife, and the Mom of a wonderful blended family of 6 children; 3 amazing elementary school kiddos, 2 wonderful teens, and 1 awesome 25 year old! She is a member of the Society of Children's Book Writers & Illustrators (SCBWI), has a Bachelor's degree in Applied Behavioral Science and is currently in Graduate school. Vania loves the kiddos, she believes the positive energy that children bring; keeps you laughing, learning, and young! Vania was raised in both St. Croix, U.S. Virgin Islands, and Seattle, WA! She arrived in Seattle as a pre-teen and has been going back and forth between St. Croix and Seattle, Washington her whole life! Vania and her Family currently reside in Seattle, Washington.

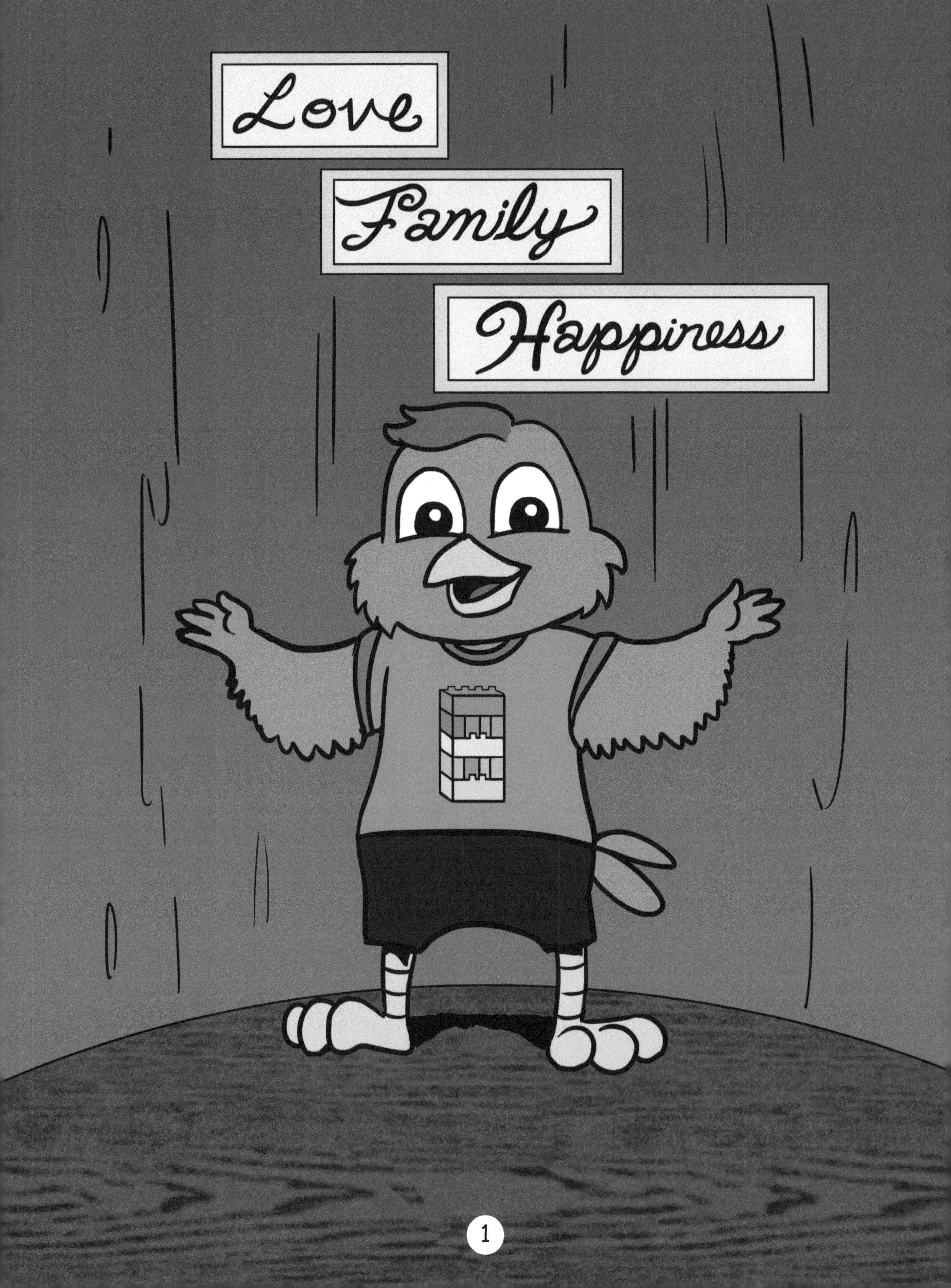
Love
Family
Happiness

I have a BIG Happy Family!
There are many different types of Amazing Families!
All families are special in their own way!
But if you have more
than 1 Brother or Sister, then you may have
A BIG Amazing family, just like me!

I have Sisters, Brothers, my Mom, Dad, and ME! We do everything together!
In a Big Family, there are lots of things that we can do to make life easier for each other;
Sharing, Helping, Cooperation, Caring and Love are just a few of them!

I don't always like to share!
Sharing can be really hard to do sometimes;
But sharing our books, toys, and time with others helps
to make us a good person from the inside out!
SHARING is our Family Value!

In a Big Family, everybody must do their part to help out!
We each try to clean up after ourselves
by putting things back in their place when we are
finished using it.
We don't always do the best job, but my Mom says we
are the best helpers ever!
HELPING is our Family Value!

In our Big Family, our house can get very noisy;
especially when we demand our own special attention
from Mom and Dad
or when we are just being silly or grumpy!
We even have our rough days when we fuss and fight
with each other;
and that's no fun at all!
Though we often forget, Mom reminds us to take our
time to calmly speak to each other,
listen, be kind, and most important - Keep our hands
to ourselves!
COOPERATION is our Family Value!

Sometimes when I'm frustrated,
I wonder what it will be like if I were the only child!
But then I remember
how amazing it feels to ALWAYS have another kid to
play with
and talk to when you have a BIG Family!
CARING is our Family Value!

Mom always reminds us of just how important
each one of us is to this Family and each other!
We are bound together with love!
Each one of us has a special place in our Mom and
Dad's hearts;
And that will never change!
LOVE is our Family Value!

Amir Navi Dad Mom Matt Mia Zaya

Asa

Yes! I have a BIG Happy Family!
I have Brothers, Sisters, a Mom, a Dad and ME!
Family is everything
And being a part of a
Great Big Amazing Happy Family
is the perfect place to be!

The End!

There are so many awesome values to celebrate!
What Family Values are most important
to you and your family?

Here is a "Family Value Award" for you and your family!
Congratulations for talking about the importance of
Family values
with your loved ones!

Sharing, Helping, Cooperating, Caring, and Love
are just a few of our favorite Family Values; what
are your favorites?!?

Family Values ★
Award

Presented To:

_____

My Family's Fave Values:

_____

_____

_____

_____   _____
Date   Presented by

CPSIA information can be obtained
at www.ICGtesting.com
Printed in the USA
LVHW01s2134150318
570055LV00011B/65/P

9 781546 229865